D0409339

EGMONT

We bring stories to life

This edition first published in 2010 by Dean,
an imprint of Egmont UK Limited,
239 Kensington High Street, London, W8 6SA

Postman Pat® © 2010 Woodland Animations Ltd,
a division of Classic Media UK Limited.
Licensed by Classic Media Distribution Limited.
Original writer John Cunliffe.
From the original television design by Ivor Wood.
Royal Mail and Post Office imagery is used by kind
permission of Royal Mail Group plc.

All rights reserved.

ISBN 978 0 6035 6517 5
1 3 5 7 9 10 8 6 4 2
Printed and bound in Italy

Postman Pat

Postman Pat's
Pirate Treasure

EGMONT

It was a sunny day in Greendale. Julian and
Meera were playing a swashbuckling pirate
game – a bit too swashbuckling!

"Watch out, shipmates!" called Sara.
"You're squashing my flowers!
Come inside and have some pirate grog."

Julian and Meera ran into the house.

In the kitchen, Sara was putting the finishing touches to her flower arrangement.

"It's the Flower Show today," she told Julian and Meera. "I won't have any flowers left at this rate."

Julian and Meera were very sorry!

"Why don't you look for buried pirate treasure instead?" suggested Sara.

Just then, Pat rushed in. "My cousin Matt
is coming to visit today, I haven't seen him
for ages!" Suddenly, they heard Matt's
hearty voice calling out at the door.
"Ahoy there!"

Pat and Matt greeted each other warmly.

"This is Polly, the ship's cat!" said Matt.

"Have you got a boat?" asked Meera.
"Please can we see it?"

Matt took them all down to the riverbank where his boat was moored.

"Wow! It's just like a real pirate ship!" gasped Julian.

Just then, Reverend Timms, walked past. "Matt Clifton!" he exclaimed. "Last time I saw you was the summer that the Greendale Cup disappeared from the Flower Show."

The vicar went on his way, and everyone climbed on board Matt's boat.

"I wonder who took the cup?" said Julian.

"Maybe it was pirates!" joked Pat.

"It wasn't pirates, Pat," said Matt, appearing behind them. "It was me!"

Matt told them
the story.

"I was ten years
old. Two days
before the Flower
Show, I took the
Greendale Cup
and buried it.
I was going to
organise a treasure
hunt and put the
Cup back in time
for the Show.
But then I got

chicken pox, and by the time I was better,
I'd forgotten all about it."

"And then your family moved away from
Greendale!" Postman Pat exclaimed.

"Yes," sighed Matt. "So it was too late
to do anything!"

"But now I've come back to find it!" Matt said happily. "Look, I've still got the map I drew showing where I'd buried it. It's on the island. That's why I hired this boat!"

"Then what are we waiting for," said Pat. "Let's go treasure hunting! Julian and I will fetch the shovels!"

"Right, shipmates," laughed Pat. "All present and correct?"

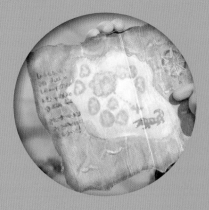

"Are we ready to set sail, crew?" smiled Matt.

"Aye aye, Captain!" Julian and Meera saluted, as they set off for the treasure.

Back on dry land, Charlie Pringle and the Pottage twins had come to play pirates with Julian.

"I'm afraid Julian's gone treasure hunting," Sara told them.

"That's what we were going to do!" sighed Charlie. "I've brought my metal detector! It goes 'beep' when it's close to anything made of metal."

"In that case, perhaps you could hunt for my garden fork?" suggested Sara. "I can't find it anywhere."

Charlie and the twins searched all over
the garden. Suddenly, the metal detector
beeped loudly over a pile of leaves.
Beep! Beep!

"Got it!" cried Tom.

"Well done, everyone," smiled Sara.
"How about some pirate grub as a reward?"

"No thanks, Mrs Clifton," replied Charlie
excitedly. "We're off to find some
real treasure!"

Meanwhile, the pirate ship had reached the island.

"According to my map, the treasure is buried near the big tree marked with an M," said Matt.

"It's here!" cried Julian.

"Miaow!" agreed Jess and Polly.

"Well done, shipmates! Right, now we take thirty paces in the direction of the fallen 'crocodile' log!" said Matt. He strode off, counting. "One... two... three..."

"I think this is it!" Matt cried. "The moment of truth. Let's get digging!"

Postman Pat and Matt dug and dug . . .

... and dug. But there was no treasure to be found!

"Where is it?" groaned Matt. "It should be here!"

"Let me see the map, Dad," said Julian.

"That's it!" Julian cried out suddenly.
"We haven't found the treasure because
we're digging in the wrong place.
The map says take thirty paces, but Matt
was our age when he buried the Cup.
His legs were much shorter then!
We've gone too far - look!"

Julian went back to the tree marked
with an M, and took thirty small steps.

"This is more like it!" he announced proudly,
and they started digging again.

Back in Greendale, Charlie and the twins
were treasure-hunting all over the village.

Outside the Post Office, they met the
vicar who was talking to Mrs Goggins.
"Will you be hoping for a prize at the
Flower Show again, Reverend?"
Mrs Goggins asked him.

"Oh yes," replied Reverend Timms.
"But it won't be the same without the
Greendale Cup!"

"The Greendale Cup!" cried Charlie.
"That's real treasure! Come on, you two!"

Charlie dashed off towards the riverbank, with Tom and Katy following.

Meanwhile, everyone was getting ready for the Flower Show.

"Still treasure-hunting, Charlie?" called Sara.

"We're looking for the Greendale Cup, Mrs Clifton!" said Katy Pottage.

But the Greendale Cup was not in Greendale! It had just been dug up by the island treasure-hunters! Julian had found the exact spot, and inside the old wooden trunk which Matt had buried years before . . .

. . . was the gleaming Greendale Cup!

"Hurray!" shouted Julian and Meera.
"We found it!"

"Now all we've got
to do is get it back to
Greendale in time for
the Flower Show prize-
giving!" smiled Pat.

Captain Matt got the boat started,
and Pirate Pat cast off.

Julian looked through the telescope
towards Greendale. "Hey! The Flower Show
has already started! Mum has won a prize!"

"Full speed ahead, Matt!" called Pat.

"And now for the Grand Prize," announced
Mrs Goggins. "The winner for the best all-
round display is. . . Reverend Timms, for his
wonderful roses!"

Mrs Pottage was about to present the vicar
with the battered old cup, when. . .

. . . "STOP!" cried Matt, marching up to the stage, holding the gleaming silver Greendale Cup.

"How... where... who?" stammered Reverend Timms.

"I took the Cup all those years ago!" Matt explained. "And I am so sorry! Reverend Timms, I would now like to present you with the Greendale Flower Show Grand Prize – the Greendale Cup!"

Suddenly, Charlie came running up, his
metal detector beeping noisily! "Treasure!
I've found some real treasure at
last!" Charlie said, excitedly.

"Indeed you have, Charlie!"
agreed Reverend Timms.
"Real Greendale treasure. Three cheers for
the return of the Greendale Cup . . .

. . . and an extra big cheer for Matt,
Pat and all the Greendale Pirates!"
grinned the vicar.

And with that,
the whole crowd
clapped and cheered
in celebration!